Carnival

of
Clouds

Works by C.H. Williams

<u>Fireside Stories</u>

Festival of Frost

Storm of Ascension

Carnival of Clouds

<u>River's End</u>

Death and the Merchant

Heirs in the Ice

Carnival

of
Clouds

C.H. Williams

ISBN: 978-1-7333569-8-5

For the believers.

Chapter 1

BRENNON

The mountains cast long, cold shadows across Old Town, leaving the hillside hovel dark despite the dawning light.

It was called Old Town because that is what it was: old as dirt. But it remained well-loved, and certainly not abandoned, for the elves who dwelled in these hills were not keen on discarding the past.

The Dradan ways were different.

Brennon liked Caelaymnis well enough. Seated by the Weir and nested in the valley of mountains, it was easily defensible and out of sight, nearly inaccessible by foot from the East.

Which meant that it was unlikely to be found.

And thus, permitted.

But Old Town, with the mossy paths winding through the trees, the ancient shelters of bark and stone built around the forest, the creaking signs above the houses that doubled as store-fronts, the quiet gurgle of the stream nearby—Old Town would always be home.

Laying in his nest of blankets atop the pallet by the corner, Brennon craned his head up, trying to see through the thin screens if anyone else was awake.

Moving awkwardly to look through a tear in the screen, he could see his younger sister Elya was still asleep, curled like a cat in the adjacent corner.

Pella was trickier to see. Daring a glance, his feet silently met the stone floor, and in a single step, he saw them. His older sibling by two years, looked to be thoroughly unconscious, one leg sprawled across their wife as the two lay smooshed on the pallet directly across from Brennon.

The sight of them both was a relic of Old Town itself. In Caelaymnis, they might've had a house of their own. But as the eldest child, Pella would inherit this house, and so, a second pallet had been scooted beside Pella's, and the family grew by one.

Brennon stifled a yawn.

Old Town wouldn't awake for a few more hours. He had time to sneak away and return in time for the morning meal—and anyway, even if his siblings noticed his absence, they weren't likely to betray him before breakfast.

Tiptoeing across the bedroom, his eyes stayed fixed on Pella.

They were a light sleeper, and of late, loyal to the notion that skipping out on the family meal was an inexcusable sin.

"Where are you going?"

Brennon started, stumbling as his foot caught the edge of the brazier at the center of the room, and he toppled to the floor, grimacing as he tried to quietly break his fall.

"Where—"

"Hush," Brennon glared at Elya, who was sitting wide-eyed on her pallet. "Go to sleep."

"Where are you going?"

"To take a piss, Elya, now go back to bed!"

"I don't believe you."

"Elya." Brennon tried to keep his words nothing more than a breath, daring a glance back to Pella. Then, looking back to his little sister, he bit his lip.

At twelve, she was insatiably curious.

And fatally loose-lipped.

Anything he told her would go straight to their parents, and at twenty-four, he was getting tired of living under constant scrutiny.

Of course, he wouldn't have needed to *worry* about the scrutiny if what he'd been doing wouldn't have been taken as a betrayal.

"I am going to tell you a secret," Brennon whispered, kneeling down beside his sister's bed. "I am in love, Elya."

Her eyes widened. "With who?"

"I'm not ready for the family to know, just yet."

"Are you waiting to be sure?"

Brennon nodded. It...was sort of true, he guessed. He *was* waiting.

Only, he wasn't waiting to be sure he was in love.

He knew he loved Olli.

He was waiting for the Carnival of Clouds.

Chapter 2

REED

Reed awoke with a start, out of breath and drenched in sweat.

Hot.

It was too hot, and she couldn't breathe—

"What's wrong?"

Pella's voice cut through the panic and confusion, their hand on Reed's arm.

Reed swallowed hard, bringing herself back to the hovel. "I...died." She glanced over to Pella, glaring. "In my dream. I died."

Pella's face fell. "I told you not to fuck with those kids."

"I was *warning* them—"

"No, you were *reminding* them, which is not only not allowed, it's dangerous," Pella lectured darkly. "For you as much as them."

Reed blew out a deep breath.

It was *one* shared dream.

And three very funny conversations with three equally confused children.

A healthy swig of elfwine to ease inhibitions, and a shared worry planted in the back of their minds, and Reed had gone to sleep a conduit. By day, she traversed the mind, and by night—at least, that night—she'd woven dreams.

She'd done it a handful of times before, much to the chagrin of those involved.

Human dreams must be different, though, for Reed had felt the reverberations of this dream echoing long after it should have departed.

It was important that the humans remember their humility.

They had no great reverence for the vastness of possibility, and Reed took no issue, reminding them that though they agreed to ignore magic, they did not live in isolation.

Simply because they didn't see the magic didn't make it any less real.

"You alright?" Pella relented.

"I'll be fine," Reed grumbled, rubbing her neck. "It'll pass." *Hopefully.* "What time is it?"

"Just after dawn." Pella's lips were pursed in dismay. "Elya's awake, though feigning sleep like Brennon told her" —a giggle came from behind Elya's screen— "and Brennon snuck out early again." They rolled their eyes. "He thinks he's being clever—"

"I doubt that," Reed put in, raising an eyebrow. "I imagine he's just looking for a bit of privacy."

Pella's lips twitched into a grimace.

It was an argument they'd had a thousand times.

Move into the city, Reed would argue. *There's work for both of us, there. You can paint. And I can study.*

Who will care for our family, Pella would snap back. *Our fathers? And Elya and Brennon, too? I cannot just abandon our family house!*

It was not an argument Reed was keen on having today, though.

Today, they would be preparing for the Carnival.

Held each year to celebrate the sacred vow made by the first Praequintelya, it was a night of revelry and mysticism, all in one.

Reed and the other Listeners would sing the clouds round the mountain peaks—or so the legend went. Practically speaking, they'd hum a hymn into the minds of those knelt in prayer, and then depart to watch the sun set over the mountains. Paper lanterns would be lit and set to drift down the Weir, fairy floss would be passed around from the sugar-spinners, and there would be wine and revelry long into the night.

And as the moon reached its zenith, the exchange.

Each Drada was permitted one votum, a humble request made in the safety of their mountain home, a request that could not be denied.

The Carnival of Clouds was all about the new.

About starting over.

Reed had done her part, making sure the humans wouldn't forget.

All that was left was to make sure her people kept their laws, and stayed out of sight.

Chapter 3

PELLA

Pella left Reed sitting on the pallet, her long brown hair silky as it lay mussed over her shoulder, pale eyes deep in thought.

It was Pella's preference to rise early, and to start the stove and fetch the water for tea. Since their marriage, they had felt the weight of family obligation heavy on their shoulders. Not that they wouldn't have started the stove and fetched the water anyway. But now, it felt...significant. A firm way of saying *this will be my house, my family, and I must tend to it.*

They did not relish going down into Caelaymnis for the Carnival of Clouds.

It would be an opportunity for Reed to push her *let's move down to the valley* agenda, of which Pella wanted no part.

The city was all well and good, but Old Town was their home. And this stone house was Pella's.

Brennon had left the door ajar on his way out, letting the smell of spring into the hovel—and, Pella thought bitterly, closing the door, the chill that clung to the dregs winter. Pulling their robe around them closer, night clothes too thin in the morning air.

Beneath the blankets with Reed, though, cuddled up close?

Perfection.

Pella didn't specifically enjoy the lack of privacy. To be honest, Pella didn't really think much of it. They'd grown up as the rest of the children in Old Town did, sharing a single room with their siblings. The stone houses had been built long ago, and it was impractical to believe that privacy would be carved into the stone. The screens were sufficient, along with a quiet word here and there, and they had never questioned it was simply another avenue of life to be navigated with respect and care—though in this, Pella felt fortunate. Most who were freshly wed vociferously sought out their privacy, with the singular aim of fucking.

The thought made Pella sick.

But it also tied them deeply to this house.

It was built to welcome souls like theirs, with gentle screens and a blazing brazier. The affection inside those walls had been built into the home.

The way Reed would pull Pella in tight. How Pella would roll over, cradling Reed, the contour of their bodies fitting together perfectly. How Reed would run her fingers through Pella's long, blonde hair, whispering about her day.

Pella sighed, kneeling before the hearth, flint box in hand, eying the fresh kindling they'd laid the night before.

There was no reason to leave Old Town.

This place was enough for them—and Pella prayed it would be enough for Reed, too.

Reed, and her restless life.

Chapter 4

BRENNON

Olli's house was beyond Old Town, past Caelaymnis, and a few hours' ride into the high plains on horseback.

But time was rather limited, and anyway, Brennon didn't really have the patience for doing things Olli's way—that was to say, the human way.

Evanescing with shimmering mist into the glade by the river, Brennon was met with the morning sun, warm across the still-dewy grass.

And he was running.

Olli's home had been dug out of a gently lilting hillside, the closest to the glade and furthest from the center of the settlement. It was a collection of mis-matched domiciles, and for that, Brennon adored the settlement. Some, like Olli's, were earthen homes—others were log cabins, others were lean-tos by the groves of cottonwoods by the river, and it was beautifully chaotic.

Brennon didn't bother knocking.

Olli's mother had assured him that their door was always open for the young Drada.

Trying—and failing—to maintain some degree of decorum, Brennon burst through the yellow door, breathless as he clicked it closed behind him.

"Brennon, dear." Olli's mother winked at him from the rounded doorway on the left before a cast iron stove, wiping her hands on her apron as she moved to greet him. "Good, just in time for hotcakes." She pulled him into a tight hug, blonde curls tickling as she kissed his cheek.

Grinning, Brennon slid off his thin leather slippers and followed her back into the congregating room.

Opening up to a row of tall, narrow southern-facing windows that let sunlight fall onto the breakfast table and a roaring fire in the hearth, the room was quintessentially human.

The table was laid with a dish of butter, a jar of sugar-syrup, a half-drunk cup of tea steaming beside a big clay pot—

"Momma, he's late—" Olli rushed in through the entry at the opposite end of the room, looking worried. His blonde, curly hair was mussed, green eyes tired, and in his rumpled trousers and loose tunic half-slouching off his shoulder, he was the epitome of cozy. He was the sort of person that should've been gently kissed to waking and cuddled beneath the warm blankets until consciousness found him fully.

Olli's look of apprehension melted, eyes lighting on Brennon.

"Sorry," Brennon grinned, meeting him halfway across the room for a hug. "Elya woke up, or I would've been here sooner—Olli, what are you doing tonight?"

"Tonight? N-nothing," Olli said hesitantly, "why?"

"I want you to come with me to the Carnival of Clouds." Brennon found Olli's hands, bringing that boy's cold fingers to his lips. "Please. Every year, each Drada is permitted one votum, one prayer that cannot be refused. With...with your permission, I would ask my parents to grant my votum of bonding."

Olli's eyes were glittering as he withdrew his hands, putting them to his mouth in amazement. "Brennon, are—are you asking me to marry you?"

"I am," Brennon grinned. "We don't have to live in my familial home, not if you don't want—we'll figure it out—but I do want them to know you, at the very least, and tonight is the bicentennial of the Carnival, it's a grand event to mark the moment, and my fathers are deeply traditional, they'll honor the votum I'm sure—"

"Love, you're rambling," Olli grinned, pulling him into a hug. "Of course, I'll go."

Brennon felt heat rising in his cheeks, half-ashamed, half-relieved. He hadn't meant to disregard the votum so hastily. It wasn't precisely serious, to most, but it also wasn't a joke. Rarely did a Drada invoke the prayer over grave matters—it would be disrespectful. To maneuver someone into action by force of tradition, to trick someone into agreement just because of a two-hundred year old practice, that was deceitful and dishonorable. But it brought a weight to argument, Brennon had found, and the question of bringing a human into the family was not a light one.

The humans living here, humans like Olli and his family, they weren't part of Aerdela. They'd struck out from the fighting, pacifists, the lot of them. And seeing as the mountain Drada had settled here in peace, it made no sense to disturb the peace.

And that meant leaving well enough alone.

It didn't involve much fraternization, unless there was an outbreak or a famine or a particularly wretched winter.

The wounds of the war were still raw, between their two people.

Then, there was the matter of nerves.

Brennon had never known his fathers to fuss over matters of the heart. But they had the peace to keep, in Old Town, and Olli's lack of Dradan talents would make his life that much harder. He'd never be able to tolerate the pitch black of the forest to take a watch-shift, or be able to hear the hearts of the family when they bowed their heads in prayer to Life and Death. He wouldn't be able to visit his family without

Brennan, or else the time and inclination to make the trek back to the settlements.

Holding Olli close, Brennon pushed the worries aside.

It was a simple matter.

Attend the Carnival. Show Olli all the wonders of the Dradan world. Then, at midnight, invoke the votum and ask his fathers for their blessing.

Easy.

Chapter 5

REED

The streets of Caelaymnis were chaotic, overflowing with well-meaning folks whose good intentions had trampled what was left of Reed's good mood—which in fairness, there had been very little cheer left when she'd arrived in the city.

Brennon had missed breakfast, and Pella was left fumbling in front of their fathers, neither of whom could have cared *less* that their son was absent for the sake of a lover, but all the same it made for a bitter beginning to the day.

Reed had hoped to find some solace, finding the city in preparation of the Carnival, and yet, as she stood in the queue of volunteers, all she had found was frustration.

The stone-hewn streets had been bedecked with paper lanterns ready to be lit, vendor stands being erected along the main road leading to the palace grounds, and it was decidedly festive, which more than anything pissed Reed off.

Someone tapped her shoulder, and that was frankly the last straw, because if one more *gods-damned* person asked why Pella hadn't come down too—

Scoffing, Reed whirled on her attacker. "What the fuck do you think—oh. Espen."

His shock of white hair was almost blinding in the new spring sun, his furs slightly muddy at the bottom but otherwise as pristine as a fresh blanket of snow. Towering nearly a foot-and-a-half above Reed, he was a monstrous man, wandering into Caelaymnis occasionally to trade rumors—rumors, and nothing else.

The man never asked for supplies, and whispers followed him, whispers that a man like that needed no supplies.

"Reed." Espen cocked his head to the side, frowning. "Just the woman I was hoping to find. Have any odd dreams, lately?"

Swearing, she grabbed his arm, dragging him away from the queue and into the shadow of a nearby alley. "*What?*"

"I asked—"

"I heard what you said," she hissed, glaring. "Why are you asking?"

Espen narrowed his eyes, crossing is arms as he assessed her. "My companion is expecting."

"Congratulations. I don't see what that has to do with my sleeping habits."

"She had this *bizzare* dream," Espen mused. "But what's weird is that she said it was preceded by an undeniably real visit from a *vora* girl named Reed—"

"Shut up, don't you *dare* say that word here, they will *riot*—"

"Reed," Espen warned. "Whatever is happening is out of control. I dislike, on principle, being drawn into the dreams of others. What were you thinking, meddling like that?"

Reed paused, eying the traveler. "Wait, you—you're with Juli? You, someone who I happen to know for a *fact* is not quite human, found his way to an Aerdelean settlement, and you have the audacity to come here to lecture me on interference?"

Espen raised an eyebrow.

"What," Reed bit.

"I'm not lecturing you on interference. I don't play by your rules, or rules of the humans, nor anyone else who took part in the Treaty. I'm here to warn you. You're playing with something dangerous, here, Reed. Do you mean for your dream to linger? Even *I'm* still pulled in, some nights. Juli dreams about it often." His expression softened from mischief into something wistful, and for a split-second, something painful and sad flashed across his eyes.

"I don't know what's wrong." Reed pursed her lips, shrugging. "The humans—"

"You awoke in my companion the Touch, you are aware of this? You made her remember magic, Reed. Not just yours. Hers, to." He clicked his tongue in disdain, face like carved stone in the relief of the alley. "I hope you know what you're doing, Reed."

"It's out of my hands." Reed turned to leave, goosepimples prickling up and down her arms in the shadow of the alley.

"You don't know how to sever the dream completely?"

"The threads are supposed to be cut with waking, Espen. I can't do anything but wake up each day and hope." She turned on her heel, glaring. "And why are you assuming I'm the one keeping the dream going, eh?"

"You need to take some responsibility—"

"What's done is done, Espen! Look me in the eye and tell me *any* of those kids are unhappy. Tell me they're in danger. Tell me that I've hurt someone."

Espen was watching her wordlessly, his expression one of grave resignation.

"That's what I thought." Scoffing, she left him standing by the rubbish bins.

"Reed?"

She stopped at the alley entrance, but didn't look back.

"Nobody has gotten hurt. Not *yet.*"

Chapter 6

PELLA

"I don't see the appeal of moving down into the city," Pella muttered, watching the tea leaves drift down to the bottom of her mug. Sitting on a cushion by the hearth with Papa, the scent of lemoncakes lingering, they were in a bitter mood.

"You think our people are best scattered across the hillside?"

"I think it is best to honor the ways that have served us well," Pella snapped.

Papa tilted his head to the side, considering the point. His graying beard was shaved close and neatly kept, his dark hair streaked with silver where it was held in a braided bun at the nape of his neck, and he had always looked a bit wild, to Pella's eyes.

Father—he had an independent appreciation of tradition, a healthy respect for things like the familial home and Old Town, and Pella had always suspected it had been Father's inclinations that kept them up and out of the city.

Yet, it was Papa that Pella found themself close to, with his flighty inclinations and fierce opinions that held unflinching in the face of opposition.

"Nothing is forever," Papa sighed at last. "The world is changing." His dark eyes met hers, unreadable.

Yet Pella recognized the look.

He had received ill news, but did not wish to spoil the festivities.

"What," Pella urged.

"You know of the Citadel," he said quietly, setting his tea on the stone floor with a soft *clink*.

Of course, they knew.

It was a relic of the Old World, sitting at the doorstep of humanity. Once a library, it had housed the wisdom of the world, and before the war, it had welcomed scholars and leaders from far and wide. It was an island of exile, the humans there complacent in the agreement that they should leave magic alone.

And to the Drada, it was a bittersweet memory that the world had once welcomed them with open arms.

"I received word from your uncle," Papa said darkly. "The Citadel is gone. It has at last fallen into the sea."

Pella's mug fell from her fingertips, shattering on the stone floor. "*What?*"

"It has been sitting untended for two hundred years, and was built nearly a thousand before that," Papa sighed, rising with a grunt to fetch a towel. "Nothing lasts forever."

Tears were stinging at Pella's eyes, tears that had nothing to do with the broken shards before her, tears that had everything to do with the deep regret of a world they wished they'd known.

"Let us speak of lighter things," Papa offered softly, gently shooing Pella out of the way to clean up the mess. "You will be at the Carnival, will you not? It's the bicentennial, and your wife has put in an extraordinary amount of work, along with many others, to ensure it is a memorable night."

Pella's words were lost, mouth dry and chest tight with grief.

Dragging themself down to the city, forcing smiles and small chat— it sounded abysmal. And Reed would use every false laugh as evidence that Caelaymnis really did make Pella happy, and it would spiral into an argument on a resentful walk home.

And Reed would curl up on the pallet that night angry and quiet, for Pella would not compromise.

Not when it felt like the world was slipping through their fingers.

Chapter 7

BRENNON

"Gods, below." Olli's eyes were wide, taking in the wonder that was the Carnival of Clouds.

The sun had dipped below the mountains, and Caelaymnis had taken to heart the mantle of being the city of lights. A moniker referring to the green and purple lights that dipped into the night sky, the Drada of Caelaymnis seemed to take the nickname as a challenge. The road was lined with glowing jars of liquid light, ribbons soaked in the stuff, too, giving an otherworldly glow to the lucent lamps tended to by the night guard.

"Alright," Brennon mused, linking arms with Olli, leading him down the street. "What's your fancy? There's prayer, which is lovely, but a bit boring—though Pella will be there, and Reed will be singing with the rest, if you fancy an introduction, but I'd counsel patience, because Pella's going to take their cue from my fathers. We could always join Elya in her quest to eat as much fairyfloss as possible, but I have found that a stomachache is not particularly conducive to the kind of loving I had in mind a bit later—"

Laughing, Olli's face went red, the way it always did when he knew he was the object of desire.

Brennon suspected that Olli wasn't a boy who was often the center of attention. At twenty-two, he seemed to have settled into quietude— or he had, until Brennon.

"What about something…Dradan," Olli said quietly, flush creeping down his neck. "I—we—could eat sweets any time. And I don't wanna make your sibling mad."

Wrapping his arm around Olli's waist, Brennon surveyed the street, brow furrowing. "Eating sweets and making Pella mad are my favorite pastimes, though," he muttered, doing his best to look dejected, which prompted a laugh from Olli.

A booth, decorated in tapers and swaths of midnight-black velvet a few stalls up caught his eye, though.

"Fancy a card reading?" Brennon asked.

Olli grinned, giving a shrug. "My gran does those. But if you like…"

Rolling his eyes, Brennon pulled Olli along towards the stall. "I really don't know what you're after—something Dradan," he scoffed as an afterthought, "as if we are creatures in a zoo…"

"This night means a lot to you," Olli mumbled, looking at his feet as they walked. "I'm trying, okay?"

Brennon said nothing. He only gave Olli's waist a squeeze, brushing a kiss against his cheek.

Olli was a man who spent his life perpetually in fear of disappointing the people he loved, and what Brennon wanted more than anything in the world was to show him how *not disappointing* he was.

The opening of the card booth was dimly lit, the awning low, so that Brennon had to duck to miss the golden tassels dangling down above the make-shift door. "Hello?"

A pair of eyes flashed in the dark, and a moment later, a small figure darted back behind the table. The air was heavy with incense, hotter and heavier than it should've been. "Pick a card," a low, hoarse voice said, bony fingers spreading a deck of worn cards out across the rickety wooden table. Brennon reached for one, but a hand slapped his away.

"Not...you. And not without payment."

"Er, what—what would you like in exchange," Olli stumbled, looking nervous.

Painted eyelids batted across wolf eyes, and the Reader cackled. But they said nothing, sliding a knife across the table.

Olli frowned, not moving.

"You have to give them something," Brennon whispered into his ear. Dradan currency was symbolic, valueless to anyone not within the enclave of elves. "They want something from *you*. A—a lock of hair, or a drop of blood, or a fingernail, or something."

"Why?" Olli asked, looking up at Brennon, worried.

Brennon puckered his lips to one side, unsure of what to say.

In truth, they'd be used for the concoctions of those who found their home in the Wild. Some wretched potion for things none ought to speak of, things that Brennon did not know or care to imagine.

Reaching for the knife, Olli looked warily to Brennon, then back to the Reader. Then, with fingers slightly shaking, he handed Brennon the knife. "I—I can't. I'm sorry, I..." His voice faltered.

Brennon took the knife and without hesitation, needled the tip into his index finger.

Metal stinging against his flesh, blood welled on the blade, a single bead running down the glinting silver, and hissing, he passed the knife across the table to the Reader.

If Olli wanted something Dradan, that meant he wanted something with *magic*.

"Here," Brennon grimaced, sucking his fingertip. "Let him draw."

The Reader's veiled head gave a nod.

But Olli stood frozen, panic in his pale eyes.

"Here." Brennon put an arm around his waist, drawing a card with his free hand and flipping it over. "There." Then, brushing a kiss against

Olli's forehead, he added, "It's okay. It's supposed to be scary."

He didn't know if that was true.

But it felt like the right thing to say, arm around that trembling boy.

Olli gave a shiver, moving in closer—and one glance at the card on the table, Brennon let out an audible gasp, moving them both back.

On the card, a single heart pierced by two daggers, a stream of blood running off the edge of the card, and—

Brennon felt nausea rising.

Where the paint gave to life, he could not say, but a shining pool of fresh blood was welling on the wood beneath the card.

"Double knives and a single heart," the Reader mused. "That can only mean one thing, darlings. *Run.*"

Chapter 8

REED

Armed with a mug of mulled honey cider, Reed was sitting on the stone steps of the palace, Pella looking miserable beside her.

The prayers had been wonderful.

Reed had closed her eyes and joined hands with those beside her, and together, they had hummed their song of gratitude into the minds of those milling about the palace steps, watching. Led by the mystics, whose order dated back thousands of years before the first cornerstone had been laid in Caelaymnis, it was both a godly moment and a moment of profound spiritual connection to this place they called home.

She could feel the wind in the pines, the dark on the mountain faces, the urgency of the river, the order of how each curve of the road came together to form this beautiful haven, and there had been tears on her cheeks, sending her voice into the harmony.

And when she'd opened her eyes, she'd seen Pella, frowning in the crowd, arms crossed.

"You didn't have to come," Reed muttered, running her finger idly around the rim of the cup. "I know you hate this."

"You are my wife. I am your spouse. It is my obligation—"

Rising, Reed huffed a laugh of derision. "I don't want you here out of *obligation*, I want you here because you love me, and because you love the things that I do!"

"I do love you—"

"Conditionally, Pella! You love a really specific version of me, that sleeps on a pallet in a shared bedroom with your grown-ass brother who's too much of a coward to tell you who he's been seeing and your little sister who is watching you both and wondering why neither of you is happy in that home!" Not waiting for Pella to follow, Reed skipped down the palace steps two at a time, cider sloshing over the side of her mug as she went.

Laughter was drifting over the top of the sound of meat sizzling over a fire, cups clinking with merriment, and Reed had to side-step a very drunk mystic, leaving the mug of half-finished cider on the stall table.

She could hear Pella's steps behind her, leather slippers scuffing lightly against the stone.

"Reed, wait—"

But she'd done her fair share of waiting. Three years of it, and sleeping on that damn pallet for two months had finally worn her down, and it took one look from Pella on this beautiful night to absolutely break her.

Taking a sharp right, Reed ducked into a house of mirrors, eager for a few moments of quiet.

And, she thought vindictively, eager for Pella to start worrying about where she'd gone.

A dozen images of herself were reflected back in the dim lucent light of whoever was tending the booth. Reed had pulled her brown hair half-up, and a flush of anger crept down her cheeks, sliding below the flared-sleeve tunic like a resentful lover.

I wonder if it scares Pella, when I dream my own death.

She'd wondered it that morning, watching Pella's eyes grow wide as she'd relayed the dream.

Reed gauged the depth of the reflections before taking a step towards the eighth reflection from the right. Fingers out in caution, they met glass.

On second thought, feeling trapped in a house of trickery was perhaps not the best way to spend the Carnival of Clouds.

Turning to leave, though, Reed came face-to-face with a reflection of herself.

The only way out would be forward.

Chapter 9

PELLA

Fuming, Pella walked the street before the palace, listening for Reed's vindicated sighs of exasperation, or else her snide mumbling of rude remarks beneath her breath.

But their wife was nowhere to be found.

Papa and Father were more than likely walking Elya through the various booths and stands, Papa with one of what would ultimately be countless sticks of fairyfloss, Father whispering tips for the many games Elya would want to play.

Brennon—he'd doubtless be caught up with his lover, enjoying the ecstasy of blooming romance.

Pella's feelings had been more than a touch hurt that he hadn't confided this in them. Them and Brennon, they'd been close, when they were younger, and it'd really only been since the bonding with Reed that Pella felt the distance between them starting to grow.

But there was a time in everyone's life when they had to step up and take some responsibility.

Responsibility for what, a voice in the back of their head demanded.

Abandoning the main drag for the quieter walk along the river, Pella ripped the question to shreds.

Her fathers were loving people. They cared for Pella, and Brennon, and Elya, and cared for them all well. Brennon could be plagued by flights of fancy, but he never neglected his duty to the house. Elya—she was young, and wild, but never cruel or unruly. Father's back was beginning to bother him if it was particularly damp or cold, but Papa had made a tincture of oils and peppers and herbs and a dash of something he refused to disclose, and it helped immensely.

Nothing was falling apart.

Nothing, save for Pella and Reed.

It had been a mistake, marrying that girl. Their disparate lives came to clash when the bond was made.

Eyes welling with tears, Pella sat down on a boulder by the river, cold stone smooth against her fingers as she sank down. The carnival-goers would be lighting the luminaries shortly, and it wouldn't be long before paper lanterns started to drift down the river.

They used to love the paper lanterns, Pella had. Forget whatever magic their people knew, *those* were the most magical sight of all.

Working magic into the world around them the way a woodworker massaged wax into the grain of a freshly-carved piece—it made sense, to them. It was nothing different than any other craft. With enough study and enough patience, the nuance would unfold and reveal the order.

But the wonder of those lanterns...

How had they stayed afloat, amid the waves? How long did they stay lit, those little lanterns?

There was no way to know if they'd ever gone out, and they'd imagined the lanterns floating down the river into the sea thousands of miles away.

Fuck that hope.

Anger was rising in Pella's chest, and the more they thought about it, the more they hated those gods-damned lanterns.

They hated this Carnival of Clouds, hated Reed for loving it, hated Reed for loving them, and fucking Brennon, and his wonderful little love he wouldn't share, and Elya, with her naivete, and Papa and Father for being so inclined to let the changing world pull their home and family right through their fingers—

The first lantern was bobbing on the water, making its way downstream towards where Pella sat.

Without a second thought, they were clamoring off the boulder, eyes fixed with hot rage on the lantern.

The rocks were slick as they made their way down the bank, the water cold as it flooded their leather slippers, icy as it bled through the woolen leggings, and with a resounding splash, Pella had kicked the lantern, sending a spray of water into the air, extinguishing the light and drowning the burned shreds of paper beneath the river.

It was no more than this fucking celebration deserved.

Clouds take them all.

Chapter 10

BRENNON

Brennon's hand was in Olli's, and he'd gone to pull them out of the tent, but the velvety arch had vanished.

"Evanesce us out," Olli whispered, holding tight to Brennon. "I—I don't like this anymore, I want to leave—"

But Brennon's magic had flickered out, he realized in a panic.

He could feel it, deep in his chest, laying dormant, suppressed by something unseen—

"Let us out!" His voice sounded desperate, dampened by the great cloth walls around them. The Reader had disappeared, and the table, leaving only a darkened archway through which he assumed the Reader had gone.

Think. He had to think, had to stay calm—

"C'mon." Pulling Olli along, Brennon turned for the arch.

He'd been to the Carnival before. He knew very well that this trickery was common-place, that the Travelers had a way with magic, and that was the *point*, to be scared. Olli's own unease was just contagious, that was all.

"Bren, I—I don't think—"

"It's gonna be fine." He paused, fingers still locked with Olli's.

And he forced himself to look into Olli's terrified eyes.

The blonde curls had been pulled back for tonight, held in a knot at the back of Olli's head, and he'd donned his best tunic for the occasion, the one that was an easy yellow, the best of summer, warming his lightly tanned skin.

He'd made a decided effort, tonight, which meant that he had already been nervous.

Brennon let the tension held between them go, relenting in his efforts to drag Olli onward. Instead, moving back in front of his lover, he found Olli's other hand and brought them both to his lips, kissing the trembling fingers. "I love you," he said quietly. "And I'm scared, too. I wanted to show you our best, and even though I know that you and I are absolutely going to make it out of this tent just fine, Oliver, you have no idea how terrified I am that you are going to hate me and everything about my life. I am worried that you are going to see this—this nonsense and be too afraid to love me, and I...am rambling again."

At this, the corner of Olli's mouth twitched in what might've been a smile. "Please, let's just...find a way out of here." Then, swallowing hard, he added, "So—so I can show you exactly how much I love you."

Brennon huffed a laugh. "That's the spirit." Then, letting one of Olli's hand drop but keeping the other held tight, he nodded to the arch.

The smell of pine filled the dark room beyond.

In the distance, the crunching of twigs and needles.

It was getting harder by the minute to believe the lies he was telling Olli.

One heart with two knives. That couldn't be a good sign.

"Olli," he whispered, "your mom reads cards, right? What do the double knives in the heart mean, again?"

But Olli's eyes had grown wide, and he was shaking his head. "Bren—"

Head snapping up, Brennon saw a figure coming towards them. A glassy moon was moving from behind the darkest clouds, and they were in an unfamiliar forest.

Pella.

"I don't know what you think you're doing with a human," Pella sneered, sauntering towards them. "Do you plan to forsake our ways?"

Brennon's heart dropped.

They were words he imagined over and over again.

"H-he's not," Olli stammered.

"Olli, no, it's not real—"

"He's not forsaking anything," Olli said again, waving Brennon off. "You—you're only used to living after the war. But my gran, she—she told me all about how it used to be. Drada and human living side by side. You're the one f-forsaking your own ways. Living alone is a new thing."

A cruel smile was twitching up Pella's face. "You don't know how badly our people hurt." They gestured to Brennon. "See how your boy bleeds."

Glancing down, Brennon frowned, watching the drop of blood welling on his still-pricked fingertip.

"You think you understand what the war did to us," Pella sneered. "You *do not.*" And with a snap of their fingers, a battle was waging, and Pella was gone.

The shrieks of wounded soldiers filled the air, the tang of blood and sweat and shit heavy in the air, and the night above them gave way to a hazy dawn.

Grabbing Olli's arm, Brennon pulled them both behind the shelter of a massive pine, backs pressed against the bark.

Or, that was what he'd intended to do.

Instead, a pair of rough hands grabbed him from behind, and a knife was at his throat.

Olli was watching in horror, and when he tried to move for

Brennon, a young human woman pulled him back. "What are you doing," she hissed, glaring. "He is *vora*. Leave him!"

"Run!" Brennon yelled, tears pricking his eyes. "Olli, go!"

But the boy only shook his head.

Brennon wasn't a particularly religious man.

In that moment, though, he sent a prayer to the gods below that whatever trickery had set this knife at his throat would leave them both alive—that this forest of fears was nothing but a bad dream.

Chapter 11

REED

The further into the maze Reed got, the less she came to like her reflection.

It was lonely, staring down images of herself. Hollow, in a way she hadn't understood until this moment.

Like a word said over and over, until it became meaningless, Reed's own face started to distort, losing itself amid the reflections.

The echo of dimples, the button nose that belonged to her mother, the dark hair that almost dissolved into the dark—

Me, the voice in her head whispered, *me, me, me, me, me, me, me, me, me* until panic started to rise.

Nothing was making sense.

Head cloudy, eyes unfocused, something had to give—

Me.

Sinking down onto the floor in frustration, tears welling, Reed pushed the heels of her hands into her eyes. Sprays of light against the pitch replaced the dimly lit reflections.

It's me. I'm giving way like a sodden straw roof.

Fucking Pella.

So gods-damned infuriating.

Reed had not intended to fall for the *ro*, the glorious epitome of everything uncontained, and nobody ever intended to fall for anyone else, she supposed, but Pella—*Pella* might as well have been wearing a sign that said Avoid Me At All Costs, because that gorgeous Drada didn't know the *meaning* of the word uncontained.

Pella spent a lot of time talking about how *wrong* the world was.

They had all the answers, of course. They knew how the world *ought* to be. And the world ought to be the stone hovel amidst the trees of Old Town.

They did not want to see beyond their tiny life. Chose not to see the paths that others might walk.

And the realization was a knife in the gut to Reed.

Pella had never really loved her.

Pella had loved the idea that they could fix her.

With an angry sob, Reed let her hands fall, the mirrors coming back into focus.

Part of her wanted very much to start smashing them. It was an easy—and destructive—way out of the maze, and then she would be free to go home and mourn.

But another, more vindictive part of her wanted to stare herself down.

She wanted to walk through this house of mirrors and fucking *revel,* because she was Reed. She didn't want to mourn. She wanted to *love* that face staring back at her, love it more than anyone else ever could, because otherwise, she'd spend her life smashing mirrors.

And a life where she couldn't even look herself in the eyes was no life at all.

Chapter 12

PELLA

Anger surged in Pella as they drowned those pathetic lanterns, flame hissing, plumes of steam rising as they buried the fire beneath the icy waves of the river.

Fuck these people celebrating, with their unrelenting joy and need to *sing*.

Melted wax froze into splays of twisted fingers that groped sodden lanterns, and Pella was vaguely aware of someone yelling at them to stop.

I am ro. I am uncontained, and I will not be stopped. They defied the gods, and they'd defy all these bastards, too.

The steam rising was beginning to obscure Pella's vision, which was an odd thing, because the candles in the lanterns didn't really burn that hot or that bright, and Pella was just one person in a sea of bright lights and there were only so many lanterns they could take out at a time—

But columns of white rose all the same, rising around them.

An intense panic followed quickly on the heels of their immense anger as the river and the shore and the carnival set up along the winding path disappeared, and it was beginning to grow hot, beads of sweat blossoming on Pella's forehead. Shapes were coming to life around them, steam coalescing into clouded figures—

A man shrouded in wisps of cloud was striding towards her, his cheeks flushed with opaque swirls of steam, eyes like candle flames.

"Why have you called us forth?"

"What?!" Defensiveness was rising. Pella had done no such thing, they'd only intended to drown the lanterns—

"You summon the votum."

"A votum," Pella snapped, taking a menacing step forward, "is a plea, and not even one offered to the gods. You mock our ways."

The shrouded man cocked his head to the side. "You are unusually defensive for someone so intent to engage in sacrilege."

Pella was left speechless and seething. The damp heat pressed close around them, making it difficult to focus. *Reed.* Maybe she'd hear. Whatever fuckery this was, it was surely one a Listener ought to concern themself with, no? Of course, the thought that Reed might be involved in this—or even that Reed with all her wildness, could *fix* this—it further fueled the agitation.

Reed was the one who flung herself onto the world in the name of making problems.

Pella was the one who cleaned up after her.

"I repeat. Why have you summoned the votum?"

Pella's jaw clenched, eyes narrow. "I *didn't.*"

"You took the blessed lanterns and sank them into the Weir. You did summon us." The man was watching her curiously, candle eyes flickering. "Unless you know not what you do. Unless..." He took a step towards her, fingers merely trails of wisps as he moved to brush her cheek. "Ah. A defier."

"I am *ro*, yes," Pella bit back.

"One whose gods-given duty is to question."

"My gods-given duty is to tell the gods to get fucked," Pella snapped. "My gods-given duty is to find equilibrium and balance."

"Where? Because I see no equilibrium," the shrouded man whispered, a faint smile on his clouded lips. "No matter. The fact of the matter remains. You have summoned the votum. And we will require that you pay the price. One soul and we will return beneath the Weir."

A soul?

Pella glared, drawing their knife. "How *dare* you claim to possess the sight to assess the balance of mortals, and then lay claim to a soul?"

The man's eyes flared, smile faltering to something dangerous. "I am Cirro of the votum. You demanded the clouds take them all. A contract has been made that cannot be broken."

"I wished for *no such thing—*"

"You are careless, Pella of the Stone House." Cirro put a hand out, eyes burning bright, skin swirling with the steam-made-man. "The soul. Now."

"Clouds take them—that's an expression," Pella spat. "It means *nothing.*"

"It means that Caelaymnis would cease to become the gleaming new city in the valley of the mountains. Clouds take them." Cirro's voice was dangerously soft. "Like souls are kept in the velvet night sky as stars, released by flame, the votum may keep the liminal clouds for our own bidding."

"What happens if I break the contract," Pella breathed.

"We claim you for the votum."

"But the Carnival would not be taken by—by these clouds, and the people there would be safe."

Cirro nodded. "Either relinquish your soul and watch Caelaymnis taken into the clouds, or join us in the votum. Give up your place in the stars and watch the trouble that is Caelaymnis ascend to the sky in service of the votum while you and your lover watch from your place on the hillside, or leave this world behind and serve the paper lanterns you so quickly destroyed. The choice is yours."

Chapter 13

BRENNON

Knife at his throat, Brennon's heart was pounding. "Olli! Run!"

Olli shook his head, eyes wide with panic. "I—I can't leave you."

The young woman holding Olli back grimaced, drawing a knife of her own. "You side with the *vora*, and I have no choice—"

"I'm not *vora!*" Tears pricked at Brennon's eyes. He couldn't lose Olli, not over something like this, not over a stupid bit of magic from a stupid little card reader at this stupid Carnival. "We're Drada! As in Dradic Triumvirate! As in, three realms allied, humanity *misunderstands—"*

Mist was rising in the forest, vociferously devouring the trees from sight one by one as in encroached on them, and from the mist, figures were tumbling forth, rolling into being from great plumes of white, eyes of flame and robes of cloud, and they were drawing swords that hissed as they met the chilled air of this nightmare.

The woman holding Olli dropped his arm in alarm. "Gods below…"

"We are no gods," one of the figures of mist menaced, their voice clear and crisp. "We are votum.*"

With a sharp elbow to gut of his distracted captor, Brennon was free. He grabbed Olli's hand and ran—though were, he did not know. The mist was circling them, a near-impassable barrier, for even Brennon's keen eyes could not pierce it…

But the alternative was to face these—these votum.

There was a shriek behind them, and Brennon dared a glance back—though as soon as his eyes met the scene, he wished he hadn't looked. The shrouded figure leading these clouded warriors drove a blade through one of the human men, and all the color began to leech from him, draining away as he screamed, eyes sparking to fire, and when he fell to the ground, he was nothing more than wisps of steam, moaning and crying in the dark.

Steeling himself, Brennon glanced at Olli. "It's gonna be okay," he whispered. "I'm not gonna let anything happen to you."

Ollie nodded, watching as Brennon pulled them both into the cover of the thick mist.

Everything went white, humid air pressing tight at them both, making it difficult to breath. But while the clouded warriors were distracted with the figments in the forest, Brennon and Olli *had* to seize their chance to escape.

That was what the card reader had said, right? *Run.*

'Course, it was a challenge to run through a forest at top speeds when he couldn't *see* anything, so they'd have to settle for a meandering and careful pace, one arm stretched out before Brennon, the other tethering him to Olli.

"Olli, what did those cards mean?" Brennon breathed, trying to keep his voice low, but still loud enough for Olli to hear.

"Two knives and one heart," Olli echoed, tense. "Er, it's...usually betrayal. That's how Mom reads it."

"Usually? Olli, please tell me there's another reading." Brennon tried to keep the desperation from his voice. He didn't want to be afraid in front of Olli. He didn't want his lover to be scared.

"Duality?" His voice cracked a little as he said the word. "Instead of two knives in the heart, it's the heart wielding two knives. A choice between two paths."

Brennon fell silent, heart racing as he took these blind steps forward, pine needles crunching underfoot.

"Bren, that…is probably why we got ambushed in this forest," Olli said quietly after a long moment of silence.

"Because living with me means you don't see your family, and living with you means I don't see mine," Brennon breathed.

"Not because of—of animosity or tension? Just…because that's how it is, when you move forward." Olli's voice was hardly a whisper, fear in his voice. "The conflict—that's you, not me. I know you're sensitive to the…the unease, because of what's happened elsewhere in Maderlav, but us being together? Bren, us being with each other isn't an act of violence on anyone."

Olli's words hit Brennon like a punch in the gut.

"Isn't it, though," Brennon asked, guilt rising. "I'm asking you to give up a place where you are happy and at ease."

"No. You're not. Because I am happy and at ease with *you*." Olli's voice was strained with worry, and Brennon could almost see his furrowed brow, would-be expression crumbling in anxiety. "But you don't believe that."

"I do—Olli, I was going to talk to my dads—"

"Your apprehension about whether you are inflicting yourself and your life on me isn't exclusive from your excitement about our love," Olli said quietly. "I just wish you'd be honest with me about all of it."

Brennon made a small sound of dissatisfaction, an irk of frustration shivering up his spine.

"Did you tell me yourself you worried about me living in the Old Town?"

"I…did, yeah," Brennon frowned.

"Okay, so you—you're excited and in love and also scared and worried? That's okay." Ollie squeezed his hand. "Let's just…let's get out of here, and then we'll figure it out, okay?"

Brennon's hand before him met velvet—

"The tent," he breathed.

Clawing at the fabric one-handed, he was scrambling to find the bottom, to crawl out. Knees on the damp earth, he was dragging Olli along beneath the curtain—

But as the mist dissipated on the other side of the tent curtain, it became apparent that all was not well. They were met with an army of clouded warriors, holding Caelaymnis hostage.

"What was that about running," Olli breathed, eyes worried, blonde hair curled with sweat.

Brennon only shook his head. "Run where? We're trapped."

Chapter 14

REED

"Reed?" Espen's voice interrupted her sobbing as she sat before the mirrors, Reed's own pained face staring back at her, taunting her.

"What," Reed hissed, seething at the interruption, pushing herself to standing. "What do you *want*—how the fuck did you even find me, here?"

Espen glared, tapping his nose before crossing his arms. "I'm a bear, Reed. It takes more than a house of mirrors to stop me. But we have a problem."

"Oh, you fucking think?"

"I do not refer to the domestic squabble you have with your spouse, though that certainly is not unrelated." Espen sighed heavily, and then grimacing, gave the mirror before them a solid kick, the entire thing shattering as it toppled, an illuminated Caelaymnis becoming visible behind it.

"That's not how mazes work."

"Reed, I do not give a fuck about how mazes work," Espen growled, taking her hand to pull her out into the street. "Look."

Figures cloaked in wisps of white, figures seemingly made of clouds themselves, strode through the street, swords drawn, corralling the carnival-goers with force.

"Surprisingly," Espen muttered, "this particular mess is not of *your* making. I know. I'm shocked as well. But your spouse has awoken old spirits, and dangerous ones at that."

Reed was drying her eyes on her sleeves, watching as these figures moved confidently through the streets, the Drada looking on in fear, or else whimpering in submission as they were escorted to the temple steps. "Dangerous. Seemingly an understatement."

"You know of the votum?"

"I dreamed of them, once. I thought it was nothing more than a nightmare," Reed breathed, shaking her head.

"They are vicious things that feed on the souls of mortals. But they cannot take them freely. A votum must be given a soul willingly. They are not free to simply roam this earth and take as they desire. There is a reason the Drada set the paper lanterns in the water to be carried far away from this place, Reed," Espen frowned. "Each lantern represents a wish that must be honored, and the votum is called when the lantern is plunged beneath the water, a signal for them to rise as flame meets water. Your lanterns are carried downstream, far past where the votum would go to seek a soul, and let the water sink the lantern beneath the waves instead of your own mortal hands. Yours has always been a temporary safety, playing with these votum lanterns the way you do."

Reed exhaled a shaking breath. "Let the water sink the lantern instead of our own mortal hands...Pella. *Fuck*." She turned, glaring at Espen. "They fucking went after the lanterns? That's what did this?" Anger swelled in her chest at thought of Pella, storming about, wreaking havoc on what should've been a beautiful ceremony just because they didn't get their way. They were *intolerable*—

"Ah, I thought you'd be interested to know," Espen mused. "The question is, what are you going to do about it?"

"Me? Why should I have to do something," Reed demanded, knowing it was a pathetically ridiculous question even as she said it. One look around, and of *course* something had to be done. It was just unfair that Reed had to do it. After all those lectures about how irresponsible she was, how *dangerous* it was to be toying with her magic so, and then Pella did *this*.

Fucking absurd.

She'd teach them. She'd show them that she wasn't the dangerous one, that her magic would yet save them all.

Storming off for the river bank, Reed let her fury take over. She'd need all the momentum she could get for this, gods willing it would work.

Chapter 15

PELLA

Pella's gaze was locked on Cirro's, unrelenting.

They would not bend.

"I refuse to believe that those are my only options," she whispered, edging a step towards him, knife still out. "Give up my own soul or give up Caelaymnis."

"As if it's a difficult choice," Cirro mocked, crossing his arms. "You cannot stand this place, that much is apparent. You desecrate their prayers—or intend to, anyhow, by plunging those lanterns into the river. You rage against them, and you do not want to be here, that much is apparent. Why else does one storm into an icy spring river in the name of ruining a such a significant ceremony?"

Maybe Cirro was right. For Pella, it *was* an easy choice. They didn't give two fucks about Caelaymnis. It was too new and too unfamiliar, too much a relic of the conflict and war, and not enough an acknowledgment of their past.

But Reed would never forgive them for giving up Caelaymnis to take to the mountains.

Perhaps together, they'd live out their years, but even if Reed didn't know that it was Pella who had sold her magnificent city of lights, there would be a grief in Reed that lived on through their years, a grief that Pella would've put there.

Then too, there'd be a grief if Pella vanished.

Right?

Maybe it was selfish to hope there would be. A hope centered around Pella's own sense of self-importance, and...and maybe Reed didn't need that, either.

Maybe this marriage had been a mistake.

Maybe Reed would be happier with someone who was more wild. Someone who was uncontained in the truest, most chaotic sense of the word. Not just someone who had found a way to balance the inside and the out.

I am uncontained, Pella could remember telling their father. *I am so full of feelings on the inside, and I must let them run free. I am not wild, I am not a risk-taker, I do not even truly want to be one seen as a righteous and holy challenger to gods, as good as that may be. I am a vial, filled to the brim. I wish to tip myself out into the world so that I do not undo myself.*

Maybe Reed needed a different flavor of uncontained. Not just someone who carefully metered out their feelings to foster an equilibrium between their own heart and their own world.

"You can take me," Pella said quietly. "Leave Caelaymnis alone."

Cirro laughed, eyes flickering. "Very good. Very good. You will make a fine votum, Pella of the Stone House. You draw hard lines in the sand." Drawing his blade, he moved quickly, plunging the sword deep into Pella's gut.

They let out a cry, falling to their knees, something like hot liquid wax seeping out from where Cirro had pierced them.

"This won't take long." Cirro withdrew the blade, sheathing it once more before he came to kneel beside Pella, hand surprisingly gentle on their head. "Breathe, darling. Breathe."

I love you, Reed.

I don't know if you can hear me.

But I love you.

I love you.

The color was fading from Pella's bloodied hands as they tried to stem the flow from their gut, their body turning to monochrome steam before their eyes in painful waves of fire and icy washes of water.

Votum.

Perhaps it wouldn't be so bad. Granting wishes, that sounded like a pleasant thing. Honoring contracts. But that didn't particularly matter, because without Reed, it would be meaningless.

At least without Pella she'd have a shot at happiness.

At least she wouldn't lose her beautiful city.

Chapter 16

BRENNON

Watching the cloud warriors pace the streets in would-be patrol, Brennon forced a calming breath out. "Okay, first thing's first."

"We need to find your family," Olli nodded, finishing the thought.

With a nod, Brennon made for the riverfront. He wasn't truly sure where any of them had gotten off to, but they'd all agreed to meet there later, and he was banking on them making the same call he did—something was clearly wrong, and it'd be best to regroup sooner rather than later.

Olli had to jog a couple paces to catch up to Brennon. "Why aren't they stopping us," he whispered, grasping at Brennon's hand, the anxiety of not being tugged along worn on his brow.

Why weren't they being stopped, indeed. It was a fine question, because the more that Brennon watched the cloud warriors the more it looked like—

"They're retreating," Brennon frowned, watching a pair roll into the mist encroaching on the banks of the Weir. "Why?"

"Maybe we never really left the card reader's tent," Olli worried.

"Maybe…" But studying the scene with narrowed eyes, Brennon sort of doubted that. He searched for any sign of his family as they approached the clouds drifting atop the cold waters of the Weir, but the chaos made it difficult to spot any of them, and the din of chatter didn't aid in his efforts to listen, either.

Olli gave Brennon a nudge. "Is that..." He pointed a trembling finger towards a figure slumped beneath a tree.

Reed.

"Fuck." Brennon took off running, Olli right at his heels.

Reed was leaning against a tree, unconscious—

No.

Her breathing was too fast, her fingers tapping nervous rhythms on the ground—

"Reed?"

Her eyes snapped open, wide and alert. "Brennon." Rising, chest heaving, she looked more than a touch disoriented.

"Are you alright—"

"No," she cut in, hissing out the word, eyes distant but holding his gaze all the same. "I...have to go. You should...maybe go, too." And without another word, she was striding towards the fog.

"What the fuck—no? No, Reed—"

"Don't follow me, Bren," she threatened, not looking behind, her pace deliberately quick.

"Where am I supposed to go? Where's Pel, where's Elya—"

"You need to stay *out of my way,*" Reed hissed, turning on her heel. "You have *no idea* what is going on here, or what is possibly at stake. Espen—"

A low, guttural growl came from behind them, and it was only then that Brennon noticed a bulking man with frost-white hair behind them.

"Reed!"

But the man named Espen had taken Brennon by the shoulders, holding him back with a firm grip. "This is of utmost urgency," he breathed, baritone voice a low rumble. "Do not stand in her way. Gods permitting, she will explain later."

And with that, Brennon watched as Reed disappeared into the mist.

"Reed!"

Olli put a hand on Brennon's shoulder, looking panicked. "She—she'll be okay? We were okay, we went through the mist and we were fine?" But the timbre in his voice said that he didn't believe it anymore than Brennon did.

"Go find your family." Espen let Brennon, eyes threatening. "If you interfere with Reed, I will make sure you pay the price."

"And who are you, making threats?"

Espen rolled his shoulders back, bristling. "Someone who does not have the patience for your questions."

Chapter 17

REED

As Reed took a step into the mist, she loosed a breath, trying to steady herself. It was dense, here, the fog tightly packed, and—

Plunk. Her foot met the Weir, ice water flooding her boot.

"Pella," she called out, voice soft. Too soft, probably, over the rush of water, but what was she supposed to do? Just *not* call out?

In the wash of white, Reed could make out faint columns of clouds giving way to a small pavilion drifting gently atop the water, mist parting way to grant some degree of visibility—

"Pella."

They were collapsed on the clouds, arm dangling over the side, fingers catching the cold water in unconsciousness.

"Pella!" Reed was moving as fast as she dared towards her spouse, slipping and sliding on the slick river rocks until she was able to climb up onto the clouds themselves. "Pella, please..."

Another figure lay in a slump on the other side of the pavilion.

Cirro.

The strain of concentration was giving rise to a throbbing headache behind Reed's eyes. A shared dream was one thing—it was to bring minds together, and give life to their imaginations. She had done it with Lilah and Juli and Grayson, had linked them in joint fantasy and with her skills, allowed them to imagine the magic that their nation demanded be forgotten. It was an easy task to do the same with Pella and Cirro.

Only now, she needed to pull Pella from the dream in which she'd given up herself to the votum without waking Cirro. This meant giving rise to a Pella who, in Cirro's dream, was convincing enough so that he did not grow suspicious and wake to find he had been swindled.

"Pella." Reed brushed their hair back, frowning. "Please."

I can't pull her out of the dream without shattering it for them both. She needs to wake on her own, and quickly.

"Pel, please?"

At last, Pella's eyelids fluttered open, confusion and pain on their face. They'd just felt Cirro drive a sword through their belly, and to them, it'd been a very real pain, one that would linger in their mind in this haze of wakefulness.

"Reed?"

"Pella, it's fine, it's okay," Reed soothed. "We have to go, though. C'mon." She pulled Pella to standing, mind elsewhere—mind living the dream that still held Cirro.

"Breathe, darling, breathe," Cirro hushed. "You have made the right choice."

It was all Reed could do to keep the image of Pella there, in his mind's eye. *"I...did," the dream Pella confessed,* though with perhaps too little fire.

Cirro's eyes narrowed. "So quick to acquiesce."

"Reed..."

"Reed," Pella whispered, confusion in their eyes. "What—what's happening? Where..." Their hand was on their belly, breathing heavy.

"We have to...go," Reed managed, gesturing vaguely towards the bank, "I...don't think I can keep him there...long—*oof*—" She'd stepped off the edge of the clouds into the river, losing her balance.

But to Reed's surprise, a pair of strong arms were pulling her to standing. "You concentrate," Pella breathed, "I'll get us to the shore."

"Ah, yes." Cirro's expression softened to something that looked strikingly like condescension. "Your lover. You'll find another. It is a painful truth that we become accustomed to all grief, in time."

Dream Pella only winced, gripping her stomach. It burned, color draining away...

Reed was only vaguely aware when they hit land again. This dream could not be broken, *could not be broken...*

"You're not broken," Cirro frowned. He pulled dream Pella up to standing, looking them over.

"I...am disoriented," dream Pella breathed, pressing their fingers to their temples. "Is that ordinary, for mortals?"

If Reed could gain some sense of where this was going, they stood a fighting chance—

"Ah, everyone is different," Cirro put in.

"Caelaymnis is safe, though?"

He nodded. "It is safe."

Dream Pella sank back to sitting on the clouded pavilion. "I need...a moment." They assumed a look of pained reluctance, and put a hand over where their heart should've beat.

"Pella," Reed gasped.

The emptiness beneath the dream Pella's fingertips echoed into Reed's, the missing heartbeat mortifying.

"I'm here," Pella nodded, arm still around Reed. Together, they were going quickly through the crowd, panic and confusion growing evermore as clouded soldiers retreated to the water—

"We have to leave. We...need to get out of Caelaymnis," Reed stumbled, words difficult to string together.

To their credit, Pella merely nodded. "Home?"

"No. Further. We need to put...distance. Lots of distance..."

"Oh." Pella's shoulders fell, eyes dark. "We're...running."

Chapter 18

PELLA

Lots of distance. I can do that.

Relief and incredulity, combined with the rush of adrenaline, was making Pella's head swim. It had been so real.

But Reed was a talented Listener, and a gifted Dreamer, and Pella felt a well of guilt that this came yet again as a surprise.

"Pella!" Brennon's voice cut through the crowd, and he was running towards them—

"No time," Reed whispered. "Go."

Reed was right. Talented as she was, even she could not hold a false reality before the votum in perpetuity.

With a pained sorry mouthed at Brennon, Pella held Reed tight, world beginning to dissolve as they evanesced them both away.

Dark woods pieced themselves together around Pella and Reed, the din of the Carnival of Clouds distant, replaced by the sounds of the forest around them. Pine needles whispered in the breeze, birds calling their evening songs, and this was not far enough. Not more than a few miles from their home.

The world dissolved again, and again, and again, and by the time the moon put itself back into the sky above them, a shimmering midnight, Pella was ready to collapse, Reed leaning heavily into them with distant and bleary eyes.

"I...can't go further, tonight," Pella panted, looking around. They had long since passed into unfamiliar territory, leaving their mountains behind for unknown forests, for rolling foothills, and at last, for these open plains that were too vulnerable.

In the distance, a little settlement sparkled with light.

Humans.

It was a risk, asking them for help. The Treaty specifically forbade it, and gods only knew if the Guild humans even remembered that anyone other than themselves existed in this world. They were selfish, and it had been easy, to Pella's eyes against their history, for those now apart of the Guilt to slide from a threat of actuality to fear to panic to hatred to distrust of fact itself.

But sympathy did not excuse them, and Pella carefully weighed their options.

Reed was beyond exhausted. To keep her mind focused was taxing, and she needed food and rest.

She'd get little of either, stranded out here.

Swallowing hard, Pella made for the settlement. The longer Reed could keep this dream going, the more of a chance they'd have. And to do that, she needed more than a cold ground and an empty stomach.

A warm cabin was aglow at the edge of the sleepy settlement, looking like the welcoming outpost Pella prayed that it would be. The Vernacular words were poised on their tongue, ready and more unpracticed than they would've liked. Olli—well, he'd only spoken broken Dradic words when he'd met Brennon, but the days that he only used Vernacular had quickly passed, for he'd picked up their language fast.

There were quiet voices from inside the cabin.

Pella paused a moment on the porch, Reed slumped into them, head on their shoulder. Fuck. Alright, here goes nothing.

Their knuckles hit the door, heart racing.

The quiet voices inside ceased, tension filling the air as steps made for the front of the house.

A man with pale blue eyes and gray-ish brown hair pulled the door open, a look of wariness turning to surprise as he looked them over. "Reed?"

"You—who are you!" Pella demanded, forgetting any pretense, a glare blossoming on their brow.

"Reed, it—Juli!" The man turned behind him, calling through the house. "Lilah! It's Reed—"

"Oh, gods...you are Grayson," Pella bit. It was those fucking kids. Reed's fucking kids. They must've been a small, subconscious anchor as Pella evanesced themself and Reed onward.

"I...am Grayson, yeah," he nodded hesitantly, glancing back with a look of faint confusion.

Hurried footfalls from the back of the house brought a young girl with curled hair and a dour expression, and a very pregnant woman at her heels.

"We need a place to rest." Pella eyed them warily. Better these children than anyone else, though, for in spite of Pella's misgivings about Reed's interference, at least they did not mistrust Reed, nor the magic.

Grayson nodded, beckoning them both inside. "Of course. Is...Reed, are you alright?"

Reed didn't answer, eyes distant.

"She decidedly is not," Pella snipped. "She requires water and food, and a bed, if you have one."

The girl named Lilah with the dour expression beckoned them both to follow. "This way," she clipped, beckoning them towards the back of the house, "Grayson—"

Grayson nodded, disappearing into an adjacent room before Lilah could finish the command.

"Keep dreaming, Reed," Pella whispered, guiding her through the hallway.

But as Reed sank down onto the straw mattress in the room at the back, her eyes flicked to Pella's, startlingly clear. "Pella..."

"No." Fear nipped at their heart, panic rising.

"I lost it," Reed breathed. "I'm so sorry. I lost the dream."

Chapter 19

BRENNON

Night had fallen, and the clouds above the Weir had not disappeared.

Brennon sat in silence on the cold ground, watching them. His fathers had gone home with Elya, and Olli had drifted off, his head in Brennon's lap, and still, Brennon could not bring himself to leave.

It must've been just after midnight when a cry of outrage broke the near-sacred silence.

Olli started, breath catching as he bolted upright.

"Shh," Brennon hushed, rising, ears prickling with the stirring sounds in the wake of the echo. Instinctively, he put his hand out, protective of Olli.

Striding through the mists was a man with fire in his eyes and a sword in his hand. "Where is she," he demanded, voice trembling with anger. "Where is Pella?"

"What is your quarrel with them," Brennon called out, wary. Out of the corner of his eye, he caught sight of Espen—or, what *had* been Espen, and what was now a great white bear, pawing at the ground with a growl.

"They deceived me—"

"Doubtful. Pella takes pride in their honesty."

"Bren," Olli cautioned, voice quavering, "the sword—"

"Olli, hush." Of *course*, Brennon could see the drawn sword, gleaming with an almost lunar glow in the night, flashing as the man held it poised to strike.

"I am Cirro of the votum, and I demand *payment!*"

Brennon scoffed. "What payment—"

"I am owed a soul or Caelaymnis, and Pella—"

"Pella is gone." Brennon straighted his tunic, rolling his shoulders back. His sibling had done their duty. They had spent their life in service of the family. They had soothed Elya's nightmares, assuaged Brennon's worries, they'd happily taken Olli under their wing, teaching him their language and their ways, they had run with Elya through the fields of wildflowers and taught her how to make flower crowns of daisies, they had talked Brennon and Olli both through their own uncontained hearts in turn—

It was Brennon's turn.

"Pella is gone," Brennon echoed again. "You can bring your request to me."

Cirro took a step forward, steaming blade pressing uncomfortable into Brennon's throat. "You? And who are you, to make deals? Did *you* sink the lantern under the water—"

"No," Brennon breathed, "but—"

"Did *you* invoke the votum—"

And Brennon was about to answer that he had intended to, because he wanted to marry Olli, and he'd been planning on invoking the votum as he had understood it, which was more of a request to his fathers than the sacred act of plunging a wished-upon lantern under water to summon a cloud spirit, but—

"No," Cirro hissed, "you did *not*. And so, my quarrel is not with you." His candled eyes flickered around, searching. "Pella agreed that they would offer themself as payment for the broken contract, lest Caelaymnis be taken entirely."

Brennon's heart clenched, mouth going dry. "They...were going to offer themself?"

"To become a votum themself," Cirro nodded, furrows carved into his clouded brow.

"I'll go."

"Brennon!" Olli's voice was uncharacteristically sharp behind him, and Brennon whirled to see a furious Olli with tears starting to brim in his eyes. "No! You do *not* get to do stupid things like run off and leave me alone! What are you thinking—"

"Pella is gone, Olli. What am I supposed to do?" Brennon meant the question, panic probably betraying it in his voice. What *was* he supposed to do, with Pella gone and this horrid man of cloud and candle talking about talking Caelaymnis?

Olli's eyes flicked to Cirro, and then back to Brennon.

Behind them, Cirro made a sound of impatience. "As...*heartwarming* as this offer is, that is not the deal. Though, in the spirit of...this attempt at making good on promises, I will give you this. Rather than taking Caelaymnis, I will settle for your sibling's agreement. I will hunt them down, and take them for the votum." His eyes flashed in warning. "If you dare stand in my way, though, you may consider this cooperation at an end. It is Pella or Caelaymnis. That is the agreement." And with that, he returned to the mist above the river, the clouds at last beginning to trail away with him, and the warriors too, until there was nothing but a lingering damp in the air and the echo of Cirro's threat on Brennon's ears.

Chapter 20

REED

Reed's tears felt unending, and though she was sure it was likely just the exhaustion, the disappointment in her chest was overwhelming.

Surely, she should've been able to hang on longer than this. With Pella guiding them across the continent in evanescent bursts, Reed had been left free to concentrate on Cirro's dream—

"Here." Pella's voice was soft as they knelt before Reed, eyes gentle. "My love, you need to eat something."

"The—the dream—"

"What is done, is done." Pella had a plate of food in hand, a hunk of crusty bread and butter alongside a pat of soft cheese, and was thumbing away Reed's tears with one hand.

Reed numbly took the plate, feeling undeserving. "I let it go, though."

"You held it for longer than most could've. Just because you could not exert the past-mortal effort or summon god-like focus does not mean you do not need rest."

Giving the bread a nibble, Reed nodded, not really believing it, but grateful that Pella would push anyway. It seemed they'd have to carry Reed—or at least her heavy heart—a few more steps this evening, even if it was just to food.

Grayson was leaning against the door frame, watching carefully.

Curious.

He was taller in person, and that, Reed considered, was why she so loved to see others in the realm of sleep, for their memory of themselves changed.

Sometimes they were shorter. Sometimes they had different hair or different eyes or looked entirely to be another person from who the were in waking, and she liked that.

Seeing possibility.

"You've...given up the dream," Grayson said at last. "What does that mean for us? Here, in the Basin?"

Pella glanced back, a look of irritation quickly taking the place of the soft expression they'd held for Reed. "I cannot say, I do not know everything, *human*. It means certainly that Cirro will come for me, and we surely cannot stay here for long."

"I know hardly anything of the votum," Reed said dully, tearing off another piece of bread. "Are they practiced at tracking? How do you move through this world when you are of the clouds?" There were many unknowns—too many, for Reed's taste.

Of course, the one question at the front of her mind was one she did not dare ask.

Can we ever go home?

And she feared she knew the answer.

Their continent had been irreparably fractured by war, and now with Cirro chasing them, it left Reed and Pella both in a particularly vulnerable situation. They could not go back, but they also would be wise not to linger here—the Guild was not particularly friendly to magic, as they considered it nothing more than fairy tale, and if the City got wind of two Drada traipsing about, spreading word of magic to those who willfully agreed by pact of Treaty to forget it...

Pella brushed Reed's hair back, resting a gentle hand on her forehead, and it was as if they could see the worry. "We're going to rest for tonight."

"You should be safe," Grayson nodded. His blue eyes lingered on Reed, though, intense.

"What," she clipped.

"We're...safe, because of you. Lilah was the one who reasoned through it. She's going to keep watch, she's fairly certain that flame against—against cloud is a one-sided battle."

"How is that because of me," Reed demanded.

Grayson shrugged. "You...dreamed us on an adventure," he said simply.

Reed settled back, picking up the pat of soft cheese between her index finger and thumb, giving it a sniff. "All I did was tie you all in sleep. The rest was you." She tossed the cheese back down on the plate, wrinkling her nose. Her eyes flicked to Pella. "I did it once with Cirro. I could do it again."

Chapter 21

PELLA

"Do it again?" Pella was staring incredulously at Reed, brow knit. "Reed, you—you're exhausted—"

"I know I can do it." Reed was rising, dark circles beneath her eyes. "He needs a trail to follow, and if we can give him a false one, I can buy us time."

Pella loosed a heavy sigh, moving to tie their hair back in low-grade frustration. "No. Not without at least a bit of food and rest on your part."

"You don't trust me—"

"I trust you completely," Pella snapped, "the problem is that you don't trust *me!* You think you know what's best, Reed. You've always got these plans and schemes, and you don't listen to anyone else!"

Reed was gazing at her, tired eyes sad. "Your reckless abandon got us into this mess," she said softly. "You were angry at me, and our lives can never be the same. Do you realize that? Do you realize that unless you give Cirro a soul, or else agree to go with him, that you will never be free? So you are stuck with my plans and schemes, Pella, unless you want to face this alone. Do you? Is that what you want, to face the rest of your life alone?"

Tears pricked at Pella's eyes. They put a fist to their mouth—

No.

No, of course they didn't want the rest of their life alone.

"You are my *wife*," Pella hissed, "why would you say such things?"

"Because you were ready to leave!"

Reed's accusation echoed off the walls, painful and unfortunately true.

"I was ready to leave because I fucked up, and I have the capacity to take responsibility for my actions—"

"You were too afraid to face this together," Reed snapped. "You were pissed about Caelaymnis, you've been on edge with me—"

"Well, it doesn't matter now, does it," Grayson put forth gently, still leaning against the door, and Pella started, having forgotten he was there. "It's moot, you're both here, and whatever happened, you've a mess to deal with."

Pella loosed a breath, turning to pace the bedroom. "Fine. Perhaps we do." They paused. "I do, anyway."

"Oh, fuck you, Pels," Reed snapped, "you're off pretending like you have to do all this alone, like you've got no other choice. Just because you've got it in your head that you're incapable of receiving help doesn't make it true." She fell down onto the bed, glaring.

"Gods." Pella shot Reed an angry look. "Do whatever you wish, but right now, you'll rest."

"They're right," Grayson put forth. He seemed to think he ought to be involved in this conversation, or perhaps he merely wanted to be here, as this seemed to him an interesting conversation to bear witness to. "You cannot fight past exhaustion. Lilah's got this, I promise."

Reed nodded, reaching for the abandoned plate of food on the bed once more. "I know she does," she said dully. She looked—well, in truth, she looked a little *scared,* and that set Pella ill at ease, because Reed didn't really get scared. She was *fearless.* Pella was full of anxiety and Reed—Reed ran fearlessly into the world.

Until tonight.

Tonight, when Reed ran into the world in spite of her fear.

Pella moved to sit beside Reed, putting a steadying lower hand on her back. "Reed, I...am so sorry that this has made you afraid, but I don't want for one moment to face this alone." Guilt was rising. They hadn't made it easy on Reed, and...and they'd pulled back hard, when she'd tried to chase the things that would've made her happy. "Rest. Eat. And then..." They exhaled deeply. "And then, dream."

EPILOGUE

The letter came on the fourteenth day of Pella and Reed's absence, addressed to Brennon and Brennon alone, and he'd taken it unopened to Olli's house on the high plains, because he didn't want to open it alone.

"They wrote," Olli said in a hushed voice as they sat on the shaded side of the house, hiding from the already-warm sun. His knees were drawn to his chest, eyes wide as he watched Brennon.

"They…wrote," Brennon echoed back. "That's got to be a good sign, at least?" He glanced over, dubious.

He'd gotten up the nerve to ask his dads for their blessing. Father had smiled warmly, and pulled his son into a hug as he whispered the blessing, but Papa—Papa had laughed, and said that it was foolish to ask for a blessing when they were so transparently in love, and that of *course* they should be bonded, and so, Brennon found himself affianced. Little beyond that had been settled, but at the moment, it was rather looking like they'd end up in Caelaymnis. It was a fair compromise, they both agreed, and it would be nice to begin something new.

"What are you waiting for," Olli breathed, giving Brennon a nudge.

Brennon only shook his head.

In truth, he was waiting for his sibling to come back.

If Pella were still here, he and Olli probably would've lived in the stone house, and invited Olli's family there, too. Perhaps they still would, but Pella's absence raised more uncertainty and questions that had yet to be resolved.

With a sigh, Brennon slit the envelope.

Bren,

I dare not mention where we're at, for I've no idea how Cirro tracks. Reed is doing her best to discern his methods, but thus far, it's been all she can do to lead him astray.

We keep the company of one Ada Follery, though, and at the moment, that keeps us far from her ordinary haunts.

I am determined, brother.

I will not keep Reed from her home. From Caelaymnis.

She tells me that you are engaged to be married—Brennon, I am very happy for you, and for Olli too. You both gain a radiant husband.

It is my fondest hope to settle this quickly, and return home to see you bound and wed to your love.

Be well, my brother.

Pella

About the Author

C.H. Williams is a fantasy author living in the Mid-Atlantic with his husband, a very spunky dog, and two troublesome cats. When not causing trouble or spending time doing foundry work with his husband, he can be found walking in the woods and listening to music. Before delving into the realms of magic, he worked as a classical musician, actively performing and conducting research about musicians' relationship to gender. He has since pivoted to legal work during the day and writing dark, contemplative fantasy at night.

Learn more at

chwilliamsliterary.com

www.ingramcontent.com/pod-product-compliance
Lightning Source LLC
Chambersburg PA
CBHW032256070726
47590CB00016B/2924